Once-Upon-A-Time

Three Prince Charming Tales

Cinderella

Snow White and the Seven Dwarfs

Rapunzel

Retold by Marilyn Helmer • Illustrated by Kasia Charko

Kids Can Press

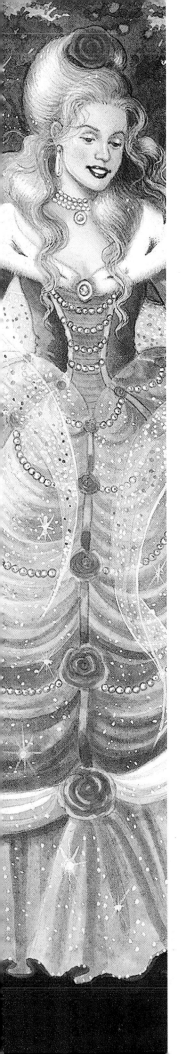

For Gary, Christopher and Jeremiah
— my three charming princes. — M. H.

To Edmund and Johanne. — K. C.

Text copyright © 2000 by Marilyn Helmer
Illustrations copyright © 2000 by Kasia Charko

Kids Can Press acknowledges the support of the Ontario Arts Council, the Canada Council for the Arts and the Government of Canada, through the BPIDP, for our publishing activity.

Published in Canada by:
Kids Can Press Ltd.
29 Birch Avenue
Toronto, ON M4V 1E2

Published in the U.S. by:
Kids Can Press Ltd.
4500 Witmer Estates
Niagara Falls, NY 14305-1386

The artwork in this book was rendered watercolor.
Text is set in Berkeley.

Series Editor: Debbie Rogosin
Editor: David MacDonald
Design: Marie Bartholomew
Printed in Hong Kong by Wing King Tong Company Ltd.

CM 00 0 9 8 7 6 5 4 3 2 1

Helmer, Marilyn
      Three Prince Charming tales

(Once-upon-a-time)
ISBN 1-55074-761-4

1. Tales. 2. Fairy tales. I. Charko, Kasia, 1949– . II Title. III. Series: Helmer, Marilyn. Once-upon-a-time.

PS8565.E4594T46 2000   j398.2   C00-930009-0   PZ8.H3696Thr 2000

Kids Can Press is a Nelvana company

Contents

Cinderella

·🎀·🎀·🎀·🎀·🎀·🎀·

Once long ago there lived a wealthy squire who married wisely and well. The handsome young couple built a stately home overlooking the town, and the parties they gave were the talk of the land. Sadly, their joy was short-lived, for the wife died soon after their first child was born.

From that day on, the squire raised the little girl himself, showering her with affection and the finest gifts money could buy. The girl grew up to be as kind and beautiful as her mother had been.

In time the squire remarried. His new wife was as different from his first wife as thorns are from roses. She was a proud selfish woman who cared for no one but herself and her own two daughters. The wedding feast was scarcely over when the three moved in and took charge of the household and everyone in it.

From the beginning, the stepmother despised the squire's gentle daughter. She made the girl cook and dust and scrub from morning till night, finding fault with everything she did. The stepsisters were a miserable pair, as ugly in nature as they were in appearance. They were jealous of the lovely girl and took great delight in making her life as wretched as possible. If the stepsisters caught her resting for a moment, they set her about the most unpleasant tasks they could think of. They threw open her closet and helped themselves to her beautiful clothes and jewels. In return she was given nothing but their shabbiest hand-me-downs to wear.

Most evenings the girl was so tired that she would sit on the hearth among the cinders, hoping no one would notice her there. Her face and hair were often soot-streaked and her tattered clothes covered in ashes.

"Look at the little cinder-maid," sneered the elder stepsister.

"We should call her Cinderella," said the younger, and so they did.

One day, news came from the palace that the King was giving a grand ball in his son's honor. All the young women in the countryside were invited to meet the Prince.

"Except you, Cinderella," said the elder stepsister.

"Oh, please," Cinderella pleaded, "let me go, too."

The younger one laughed. "Imagine you at a ball! You would shame us with your ragged clothes and dirty face."

Cinderella held back her tears. She said nothing more, but in her heart she dreamed about going to the ball.

On the day of the ball, the stepsisters were even more disagreeable than usual. They screeched and complained until the house echoed with their shrill voices. "Cinderella, let out the seams of my velvet gown!" "Where is my diamond necklace?" "Stitch my petticoat!" "Curl my wig!"

Cinderella didn't have a moment's rest until the stepsisters climbed into their coach. Away they went, arguing and bickering, without so much as a backward glance.

Cinderella collapsed on the hearth. "If I had just one wish," she murmured, "I would wish to go to the ball."

"Your wish will be granted, my child," a voice whispered in her ear.

Startled, Cinderella looked up. Beside her stood a lady dressed in silver and white, holding a sparkling crystal wand. "I am your Fairy Godmother," she said. "Tonight you will dance at the grand ball. Hurry now, we haven't a moment to waste."

Cinderella scrambled to her feet.

"Bring me the biggest pumpkin you can find," said the Fairy Godmother.

Cinderella hurried out to the pumpkin patch and picked the finest one there. The Fairy Godmother waved her crystal wand. With a flash, the pumpkin turned into a golden coach.

"Now," said the Fairy Godmother, "bring me the mousetrap from the pantry."

Cinderella brought the trap. When she opened it, six white mice and a large black rat scurried out. With a flick of the wand, the mice became six prancing horses.

"Wouldn't he make a fine coachman?" asked Cinderella, pointing to the rat. *Flick!* The rat turned into a handsome coachman.

Cinderella looked down at her shabby clothes. Once more the Fairy Godmother waved her wand. As Cinderella watched in wonder, her ragged dress turned into a flowing satin gown trimmed with ermine and pearls. On her feet were slippers of the finest spun glass.

"Off to the ball you go," said the Fairy Godmother. "But remember, you must be home by midnight. On the last stroke of twelve, your coach will turn back into a pumpkin and your dress into rags. Everything will be as it was before." Cinderella kissed her Fairy Godmother, climbed into the golden coach and sped away to the palace.

A hush fell as the beautiful stranger entered the ballroom. All eyes were upon Cinderella but no one recognized her, not even her stepsisters.

So entranced was the Prince by her beauty that he couldn't take his eyes off her. With a courtly bow, he asked Cinderella to dance. She nodded and the Prince drew her into his arms. Scarcely aware of the music or the guests around them, Cinderella and the Prince danced on and on.

Suddenly the tower clock boomed out the first stroke of midnight. With a gasp Cinderella remembered her Fairy Godmother's warning. She spun away from the Prince and dashed out of the ballroom. As she ran down the steps to her coach, Cinderella stumbled. One of her little glass slippers came off but she didn't dare stop to pick it up.

The Prince raced after her. When he reached the steps, Cinderella had vanished. Then he noticed the little slipper. He picked it up and held it next to his heart. "I will find the girl whose foot fits this slipper," he vowed. "It is she whom I love and she whom I will marry."

The next day news went out that the Prince was searching for the owner of the glass slipper. Every woman in the kingdom was to try it on.

When the royal messenger arrived at Cinderella's house, the stepsisters argued and bickered over who would try on the slipper first. Of course it didn't matter. Regardless of how they pushed and pulled, neither one could get her foot into the delicate slipper.

"May I try?" Cinderella asked.

"You?" said the elder stepsister scornfully.

"It would be a waste of time," snapped the younger.

The messenger spoke up. "The Prince declared that every woman must try on the slipper."

The stepsisters watched in amazement as Cinderella slid her foot easily into the glass slipper. She took its mate from her pocket and slipped it on, too. At that moment, the Fairy Godmother appeared. With a wave of her crystal wand she turned Cinderella's rags into a jeweled gown of the finest silk brocade. For the first time in their lives, the stepsisters were speechless.

Through the open window came the sound of horses' hoofs as the golden coach appeared once more. Cinderella climbed in and rode off in splendor to meet the Prince. They were married soon after and lived a long and happy life together.

The stepsisters came to live at the palace too, and they were as nasty and miserable as they had ever been. They spent their days sitting by the hearth, arguing and bickering, waiting for *their* fairy godmother, who never came.

Snow White and the Seven Dwarfs

Once upon a time, when the land was white with snow, a beautiful Queen sat sewing by her ebony-framed window. As she leaned out for a breath of air, the needle pricked her finger. Three drops of crimson blood fell onto the snow-covered sill.

"How pretty the colors are," the Queen said to herself. "If only I could have a daughter with skin as white as snow, lips as red as blood, and hair as black as ebony." Not long after, the Queen gave birth to the child she had wished for and named her Snow White.

When Snow White was just three days old, her mother died. Her father soon remarried, but the new Queen was a cold jealous woman who prized her beauty above all else. She had a magic mirror and she often stood before it and asked:

> *Mirror, Mirror, wise and grand,*
> *Who is the fairest in the land?*

The mirror always replied:

> *Of all the beauties ever seen,*
> *You are the fairest, Lady Queen.*

These words brought a smile to the Queen's lips, for the mirror always spoke the truth.

By her fifteenth birthday, Snow White was so beautiful that all who saw her remarked on her loveliness. And that very day, when the Queen again asked her mirror the same question, the mirror replied:

Though fair you are, my Lady Queen,
Snow White is the fairest one I've seen.

The Queen's face turned green with envy and her eyes flashed with hatred. She couldn't bear to think that there was anyone lovelier than she. Summoning her royal huntsman, she ordered, "Take Snow White far away and see to it that she never returns."

The huntsman dared not disobey the Queen. He took Snow White deep into the forest, where the trees grew so close together that scarcely a glimmer of light passed between them. Since he could not bring himself to kill the child, he left her there, knowing that she would never find her way home.

Alone and lost, Snow White wandered deeper and deeper into the forest. Everywhere she looked dark shadows loomed. From the silent trees, eyes like glowing embers seemed to be watching her.

Terrified, Snow White ran until she came to the edge of the gloomy forest. Ahead was a clearing, and beyond that rose a high mountain. The late afternoon sun shone on its peak, turning the snow-covered tip to gold. At the foot of the mountain stood a small cottage.

Snow White knocked on the door but no one answered. Needing somewhere to rest, she pushed the door open and went inside.

She found herself standing in a bright cheery room. At one end was a long low table set with seven plates and goblets. On a small stove in the corner, a pot of stew simmered, filling the air with a tantalizing smell. Too hungry to resist, Snow White helped herself to one small bowlful.

When she finished, she washed the bowl and put it away. Then she went into the next room. In it were seven small beds, each covered with a soft quilt. "I'll just lie down for a minute," Snow White told herself. Before she knew it, she was fast asleep.

As the sun set over the golden mountain, seven little men returned to the cottage. They were astonished to find a beautiful young girl asleep on one of their beds. Snow White was just as astonished to wake and find the seven dwarfs staring at her.

"Don't be afraid, child," said the first.

"Tell us who you are," said the second.

"What are you doing here?" asked the third.

Snow White told the dwarfs about her stepmother and how the huntsman had abandoned her in the forest.

"You're most welcome to stay with us," the dwarfs said kindly. "But you must beware of the wicked Queen, for she will soon know where you are. Never let anyone into the house while we're away."

So Snow White stayed with the seven dwarfs. Each day she cooked the meals and cleaned the cottage. In the evening she sat by the fire, listening to the tales the dwarfs loved to tell.

Back at the palace, believing that Snow White was dead, the Queen once again asked her mirror:

Mirror, Mirror, wise and grand,
Who is the fairest in the land?

And the mirror replied:

Though fair you are, my Lady Queen,
Snow White is the fairest one I've seen.
With seven dwarfs she lives today
Near the golden mountain, far away.

The Queen shook with rage, but she quickly gathered her wits about her. Hurrying to the orchard, she picked a basket of apples. She chose a fine one, white as snow on one side and red as blood on the other. Her eyes gleamed with malice as she dipped the red half into a poisoned brew. Then, disguised as a peasant woman, she made the long journey to the cottage of the seven dwarfs.

"Taste my crisp apples," she called as she knocked on the door.

"I can't come outside, nor can I let you in," Snow White called back to her.

"Then come to the window, my dear," coaxed the clever Queen. "I'll share an apple with you."

Intrigued, Snow White opened the window. The Queen cut the poisoned apple in two and took a bite from the white half. She offered the blood-red half to Snow White.

The instant Snow White tasted the apple, a chunk slipped into her throat and cut off her breath. She sank to the floor and lay as still as death.

There was great sorrow when the dwarfs returned that evening and found Snow White. Grief-stricken, they laid her in a glass coffin and placed it on the mountainside in a meadow of wildflowers.

It happened one day that a Prince rode by and saw the coffin. So enchanted was he by Snow White's beauty that he returned each day to sit and gaze at her.

"Let me take the coffin back to my palace so that I can keep her with me always," he begged the dwarfs. Reluctantly they agreed, for they could see how much the Prince loved Snow White.

As the Prince's footmen lifted the coffin, one of them stumbled. The jolt dislodged the poisoned apple from Snow White's throat and she began to breathe again. She opened her eyes and looked into the face of the handsome Prince.

The Prince took her in his arms and told her everything that had happened. Then he promised to cherish and protect her always. As she listened to his tender words, Snow White knew that she loved him, too. They were married soon after and lived together in happiness until the end of their lives.

And what of the wicked Queen? On the day of Snow White's wedding, the Queen once again asked her mirror:

> *Mirror, Mirror, wise and grand,*
> *Who is the fairest in the land?*

And the mirror replied:

> *Though fair you are, my Lady Queen,*
> *Snow White is the fairest one I've seen.*
> *Today she'll be the Prince's bride*
> *And rule the kingdom at his side.*

Overcome with rage, the Queen smashed the mirror into a thousand pieces. Now there was no one to tell her whether she was the fairest in the land or not, so the Queen never knew a moment's peace for the rest of her days.

Rapunzel

There was once a young couple who joyfully awaited the birth of their first child. To pass the time, the woman often sat at her bedroom window and looked down into her neighbor's garden. Strange and exotic plants bloomed in profusion behind the high stone wall. No one had the courage to enter the garden because it belonged to an evil Witch. Yet the young wife felt herself drawn to it as the tide is drawn to the moon.

One day she spotted a patch of delicious purple rapunzel growing just inside the wall. She was overcome by such a powerful craving for the plant that she rushed to her husband and begged him to bring her some.

Her husband stared at her, aghast. "I dare not go into the Witch's garden, let alone steal her plants!" he cried. "Goodness knows what evil would befall us."

"I will die if I don't get some," the young wife pleaded. Indeed, she did look as pale as death.

The husband loved his wife dearly and he could not bear to see her so distraught. That evening he climbed over the wall and picked a handful of rapunzel.

As soon as he returned, his wife made a salad with it. She ate it so quickly she almost choked. Like magic, color flowed back into her cheeks. "Oh, Husband, I must have more," she said.

Again the husband climbed over the wall, but this time the Witch was waiting for him.

"Thief!" she shrieked at the terrified young man. "How dare you sneak into my garden and steal what is mine?"

The husband fell to his knees and begged her forgiveness. "I did this for the sake of my wife and the child she will soon bear," he pleaded. "Please let me go!"

The Witch's eyes glittered like shards of ice. "I will let you go on one condition," she said. "In exchange for the rapunzel, you must give me the child."

So anxious was he to escape that the husband agreed, not believing for a moment that the Witch would hold him to his promise. But on the very day their daughter was born, the Witch came to claim her.

"By rapunzel she is mine, so Rapunzel shall be her name," she said. She snatched the child from the arms of the horrified parents and took her far away.

The years passed and Rapunzel grew. There was not a fairer maiden in all the land. She was tall and graceful, with hair that hung down her back in shining golden braids. On Rapunzel's twelfth birthday, the Witch took her deep into the forest and locked her in a high stone tower. The tower had neither stairway nor door, just one small window that looked out over the treetops.

Each day at dusk, the Witch came to visit. She would stand at the bottom of the tower and call out:

> *Rapunzel, Rapunzel, let down your hair,*
> *That I may climb its golden stair.*

The moment she heard the Witch's voice, Rapunzel wound her thick golden braids around the window hooks and let them down to the ground. Hand over hand, the Witch climbed up. Rapunzel always welcomed her, because the Witch was the only company she had.

When she was alone, Rapunzel often sang to herself to pass the time. She had a voice as clear and as lovely as a nightingale's call.

One evening a Prince was riding through the forest. When he heard Rapunzel's singing, he followed the sound until he came to the lonely tower. Just then the Witch stepped out of the shadows. The Prince hid among the trees and listened as she called out:

Rapunzel, Rapunzel, let down your hair,
That I may climb its golden stair.

He watched, amazed, as a maiden appeared in the window. She was more beautiful than any the Prince had seen before. As she leaned out, her long golden braids tumbled to the ground. Hand over hand, the Witch climbed up and disappeared inside.

The Prince never took his eyes from the window while he waited for the Witch to leave. The moment she was gone, he stood at the bottom of the tower himself and called out:

Rapunzel, Rapunzel, let down your hair,
That I may climb its golden stair.

The golden braids swung down and the Prince climbed up. As he stepped into the tower room, it was Rapunzel who gazed in amazement, for she had never seen a living person other than the Witch. She was frightened at first, but the Prince spoke so gently and looked at her so adoringly that Rapunzel found herself falling in love with him.

"We must think of a way for you to escape from the tower so we can be together forever," said the Prince.

"I have an idea," said Rapunzel. "Each time you visit me, you must bring a skein of the strongest silk you can find. We will weave the skeins into a ladder so that I can climb down to you."

From then on, the Prince came every morning. Each time he brought another skein of silk, and together he and Rapunzel worked at weaving the skeins into a ladder.

All went well until one evening when Rapunzel, forgetting herself, said to the Witch, "Good Dame, why does it take you so much longer to climb up to me than it does my Prince?"

The Witch let out a scream of rage and, taking a pair of scissors from her pocket, snipped off Rapunzel's hair. Muttering a few magic words, she banished the girl to a distant desert. Then the Witch tied the golden braids to the window hooks and waited for the Prince to come.

By and by she heard him call out:

> *Rapunzel, Rapunzel,*
> *let down your hair,*
> *That I may climb*
> *its golden stair.*

Once again the braids swung down and the Prince climbed up, expecting to see his beloved Rapunzel. To his horror, he found the Witch waiting instead.

"She's gone!" shrieked the Witch. "You'll never see your true love again." With a mighty push, she sent the Prince hurtling from the window into the thorn bushes below. The bushes broke his fall, but the thorns scratched his eyes, blinding him.

For years the Prince wandered, sad and alone, over mountains, through forests and across barren plains. Then one glorious day he heard again the sweet song that had drawn him to the lonely tower so long ago. The Prince had come to the desert where Rapunzel now lived.

Rapunzel could not hold back tears of joy as she ran to embrace him. Two tears fell from her cheeks into the Prince's eyes. Instantly

his sight was restored. Together, Rapunzel and the Prince journeyed long and far, back to the Prince's kingdom. There they were married and one day twin children, a boy and a girl, were born to them. They all lived happily ever after, ruling the kingdom in peace and contentment.